W9-ARL-092

Jane Clarke
illustrated by Britta Teckentrup

LEAP FROG

nosy crow™
An imprint of Candlewick Press

The three bullfrogs in this jungle pool are all making lots of noise. But one small frog is not joining in. Can you spot him?

Good job! You've found Felix!

Felix is a tree frog. Tree frogs don't live in ponds like most other frogs. They live high in the branches of jungle trees. Felix must be lost.

But wait . . .
Did you hear that?

Plip! Plop! Splash!

What's that noise?

Felix looks worried, doesn't he?
Let's turn the page and show him there's
nothing to be scared of.

It's just a friendly turtle popping up
to watch the sunset.

She gave Felix such a fright that he hid
behind a bumpy rock!

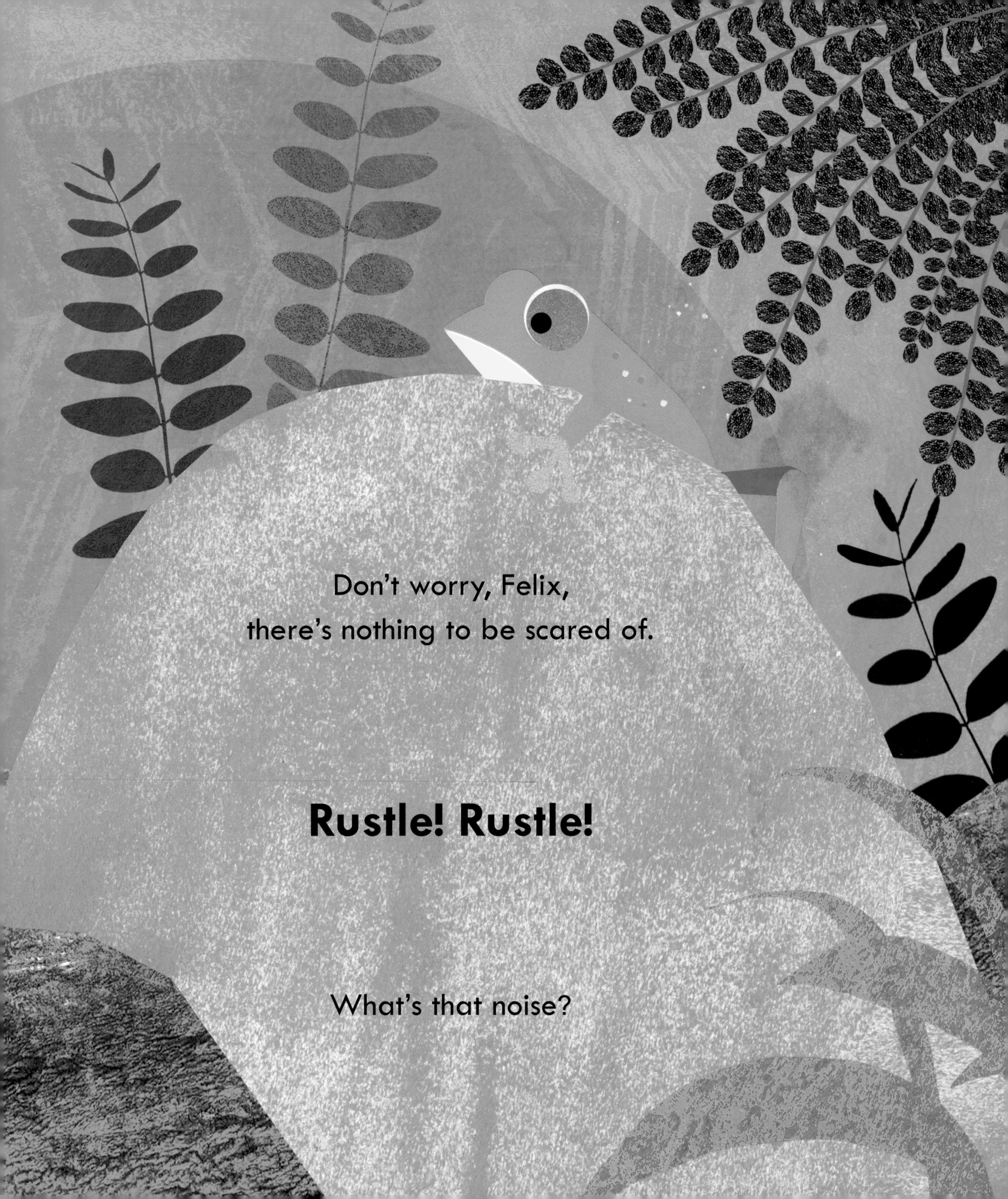

Don't worry, Felix,
there's nothing to be scared of.

Rustle! Rustle!

What's that noise?

It's just a shiny beetle walking
across the leaves.

But Felix has already leaped away down the path.

Don't worry, Felix, there's nothing to be scared of.

Crack! Crunch!

What's that noise?

It’s just the playful monkeys
nibbling their nutty nighttime snacks
and throwing down the shells.

Poor Felix. He's a very jumpy frog, isn't he? He has leaped off again.

Don't worry, Felix, there's nothing to be scared of.

But I hope we don't hear any more strange sounds.

Swish-slither!

Uh-oh! What's that noise?

It’s a slithery snake
searching for a bite to eat.

Clap your hands
and shout,
“Shoo, slithery snake!”

Hooray! You scared the snake away.

That was scary!
Maybe the jungle floor is a little dangerous for a tree frog.
Would Felix be safer in the trees?

Felix must have had the same idea. He's starting to climb.

Up . . . up . . . up he goes!

But . . .

Rat-a-tat-tat!

What's that noise?

Phew! It's only a busy woodpecker
tap-tapping on the tree trunk.

He's nothing to be scared of. But Felix
is climbing faster now, up the tree.

It's a very tall tree,
but Felix's sticky toes
help him climb.

Let's count the branches
as he climbs.

At last! He has reached the top of the tree.
Well done, Felix.

Hop! Hop! Hop!

What's that noise?

It's getting closer . . . and closer . . . and closer . . .

Something's coming!

We need to warn Felix!

Leap, frog!

Ah! Felix knows there's nothing to be scared of.

It's his daddy!

It's time for bed, and Felix's daddy has come to say good night.

Now the jungle is peaceful and quiet.

Sweet dreams, Felix.

For Pippa, with love
J. C.

To Rolf-Arne
and Astrid
B. T.

First U.S. edition 2020

Library of Congress Catalog Card Number pending
ISBN 978-1-5362-1205-1

19 20 21 22 23 24 WKT 10 9 8 7 6 5 4 3 2 1

Printed in Shenzhen, Guangdong, China

This book was typeset in Tw Cen MT Pro.
The illustrations were created digitally.

Nosy Crow
an imprint of
Candlewick Press
99 Dover Street
Somerville, Massachusetts 02144

www.nosycrow.com
www.candlewick.com